KU-756-580

The FOOT BOOK

By

Dr. Seuss

COLLINS

Trademark of Random House, Inc., William Collins Sons & Co. Ltd., Authorised User

CONDITIONS OF SALE
The paperback edition of this book is sold subject to the condition that it shall not, by way of trade or otherwise, be lent, re-sold, hired out or otherwise circulated without the publisher's prior consent in any form of binding or cover other than that in which it is published and without a similar condition including this condition being imposed on the subsequent purchaser.

5 6 7 8 9 10

ISBN 0 00 171274 8 (paperback)
ISBN 0 00 171202 0 (hardback)

Copyright © 1968 by Random House, Inc.
A Bright and Early Book for Beginning Beginners
Published by arrangement with
Random house, Inc., New York, New York
First published in Great Britain 1969

Printed in Great Britain by
William Collins Sons & Co Ltd, Glasgow

Left foot
Left foot

Right foot
Right

Feet in the morning

Feet at night

Left foot
Left foot
Left foot
Right

Wet foot

Dry foot

High foot
Low foot

Front feet

Back feet

Red feet

Black feet

Left foot Right foot

Feet Feet Feet

How many, many
feet you meet.

Slow feet

Quick feet

Trick feet

Sick feet

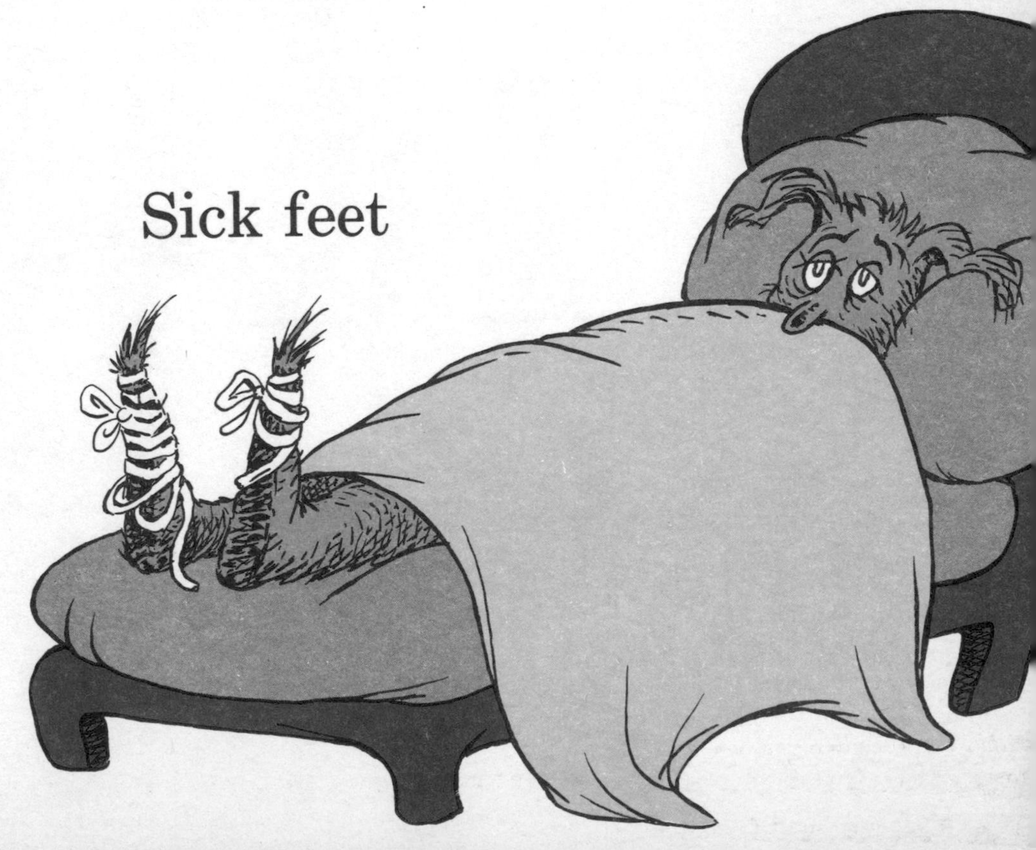

Up feet

Down feet

Here come clown feet.

Small feet

Big feet

Here come pig feet.

His feet

Her feet

Fuzzy fur feet

In the house,
and on the street,

how many, many
feet you meet.

Up in the air feet

Over a chair feet

More and more feet

Twenty-four feet

Here come
more and more . . . .

. . . . and more feet!

Left foot. Right foot.

Feet. Feet. Feet.

Oh, how many
feet you meet!